Published by Modern Publishing
A Division of Unisystems, Inc.,
under License by Joseph A. Marino Design Associates.

Printed in Singapore

A PLACE
OF OUR OWN

Written and Illustrated by Susan Marino

MODERN PUBLISHING
A Division of Unisystems, Inc.
New York, New York 10022

Sunny Side Up and Egg Nog were very unhappy. They had just set up their train set. The track was lined up just right and all the cars were out and ready to roll when their mother entered the room. "It's time to clean up," she said.

"That's not fair," Sunny Side Up whined. "Why do we have to keep our room neat and clean?"

"We'll just take out our toys again after we've put them away," Egg Nog added.

"What's up you guys?" Hard Boiled asked as he entered his younger brothers' room.

"Mom said we have to clean up," Egg Nog said.

Hard Boiled glanced around the cluttered room. "You have to admit it is a little messy," he said. "I don't know how you two can find your beds under all this stuff. 'Specially when it's dark."

"Well, there just isn't enough room in here for us to play with all of our toys," Sunny Side Up grumbled.

"Hey, you guys! I have an idea," Hard Boiled said with a grin. "How would you like a special place to play that never has to be cleaned up?"

"That would be great!" Sunny Side Up shouted.

"But where is it?" Egg Nog asked.

Hard Boiled pointed out the window. "What if we build you a clubhouse in the backyard?" he said. "You could play there, and you could invite all your friends to join, too."

"What a super idea!" Egg Nog said as he jumped up and down.

"Let's get started right away!" Sunny Side Up said, as he jumped even higher.

Early the next morning, Sunny Side Up, Egg Nog and Hard Boiled hurried to their backyard. They were ready to begin building the clubhouse. They had everything they needed. There were hammers, nails, planks, boards, paint and brushes.

However, even though the brothers worked and worked, the clubhouse was far from finished.

"I'm hungry," Egg Nog said as he collapsed on the lawn.

"It's lunchtime," Hard Boiled said. "You can take a break, but don't take too long because the more time you waste, the longer it will take to finish the clubhouse."

The back door opened and Egg Salad, the boys' sister, called to them. "Lunch is ready," she said. Egg Cream, her best friend, was with her.

"Let's have a quick sandwich to keep up our strength," Hard Boiled said. "Then we can get back to work."

"That's a good idea," Egg Nog said.

Later Egg Salad and Egg Cream asked Hard Boiled what he was doing. "I'm helping Sunny Side Up and Egg Nog build a clubhouse. You two can be the first members."

Sunny Side Up dropped his sandwich. Egg Nog's eyes popped open wide.

"Hey, that's crazy," Sunny Side Up said.

"We never play with girls," Egg Nog added.

Egg Salad was puzzled, too. "What's the catch?" she asked. "You never wanted us to play with you before."

"Well, I think it's about time we all played together," said Hard Boiled as he shuffled from one foot to the other. "And, uh, we could use a little help building the clubhouse, too."

"I knew there was a catch," Egg Salad laughed. She winked at her best friend. "We'll help, won't we, Egg Cream?"

"Sure," Egg Cream said with a grin.

The afternoon flew by. With five eager workers pitching in, the little building soon looked like a real clubhouse.

Hard Boiled was putting the finishing touches on the door when his friend Over Easy walked by.

"Hey, Hard Boiled," Over Easy called. "What are you up to?"

Hard Boiled stepped back. "I'm helping my brothers and sister build a clubhouse," he said. "It'll be finished just as soon as I hang this door." He pushed and shoved, but he couldn't get the door to fit.

"Let me help," Over Easy offered as he picked up a hammer and pounded in a nail that was sticking out. "That should do it," he said with a satisfied smile.

Egg Nog had been watching. "Gee, thanks for the help," he said.

Sunny Side Up was pleased too. "Say, Over Easy, would you like to join our club?"

Over Easy was thrilled. "I sure would," he said. "It would be great to be in a club with a bunch of Scrambled Eggs."

"Scrambled Eggs!" Egg Nog said. "What do you mean by that?"

Over Easy pointed to each one in the group. "It's a club that's open to everyone," he explained. "It doesn't matter if you're a boy or a girl or how old you are. All that counts is that you are willing to help."

Everyone agreed with Over Easy. They all pitched in and made a big sign to hang over the clubhouse door. "Scrambled Eggs," it read.

"And everyone is welcome!" shouted all the Scrambled Eggs.